How to be a brilliant writer!

By J. Alexander

A & C Black • London

We would like to thank Calum Gilligan, Louisa Goodfellow
and Joseph Knight for their help in reviewing this book.

First published in 2005 by
A & C Black Publishers Ltd
37 Soho Square, London W1D 3QZ

www.acblack.com

Design by Giraffic Design
Edited by Mary-Jane Wilkins

ISBN 0-7136-7380-X `

A CIP catalogue for this book is available
from the British Library.

A & C Black uses paper produced with elemental chlorine-free
pulp, harvested from managed sustained forests.

Printed in Great Britain by Creative Print and Design, Ebbw Vale.

Contents

It's no use! *We have a*

Once upon a time **Splis**

Thank you AT LAST *Did you see*

Oh no! *tiny*

unless...

" "

No!

I was bored

what a cleverclogs If only

One day ●amazing

gasp

She let out a gasp

I must tell you

HELP!

My heart sank

Best wishes

AH!

*

fant

she took

not in a million ye

♥ POWERFUL *Ho*

Later that evening! sa YES

... and prompty fell in

Part One

Who can?
You can!

1. What is a brilliant writer?

Most people think you can tell who's a brilliant writer by the grades they get in school. But that's not always the case. Meet Harry, Emma, Jade and Peter. Three are brilliant writers – but it may not be the three you think.

To find out which are the brilliant writers, you need to check out the writing they're doing when they aren't at school.

Being a brilliant writer isn't about getting great grades in school – it's about using and enjoying writing as an important part of your whole life, like Emma, Jade and Peter.

Why bother?

Does it sound like hard work? Don't worry! Learning to play a musical instrument or following a football team takes a lot of effort, but you hardly notice it because you're enjoying yourself and getting a lot out of it.

Here are some of the things you can get out of being a brilliant writer –

Author tip

What's so good about writing?

1. Being able to murder people at will and get away with it.

2. Becoming the best-looking fantastic footballer on the planet.

3. Getting paid for daydreaming.

Malcolm Rose, author of *The Tortured Wood* (Usborne Thrillers, 0-7460-6035-1) www.malcolmrose.co.uk

1. It's fun!

Being a writer means playing around with ideas in your imagination and using them to make something completely new. Younger kids do it all the time in pretend games, and people of every age do it in their daydreams and fantasies.

Because you don't need anyone else to help you, being a writer is also a top cure for loneliness and boredom.

2. It helps you sort out bad stuff

It helps you understand your feelings better and work out the best way of dealing with problems so you don't drown in floods of tears or bash someone up.

3. It makes you feel good about yourself

Writing's like everything else – the more you do it, the better you get – and the better you get at anything, the better you feel about yourself.

4. It boosts your brain power

Most writing involves looking for new ideas, sifting out what's important and putting it all together.

5. It connects you with other people

Sharing writing with your mates is a great way of having a laugh or a heart-to-heart. Sharing your ideas with people you don't know, like writing to your local MP, means you can make a difference in the world.

You don't have to take my word for it – just start writing! Find out for yourself what being a writer can do for you.

What if you're not good enough?

Obviously, you need some basic writing skills.
Do this little test to see if you've got them.

THE LITTLE SKILLS TEST

1. Get a pen and paper.

2. Think of something you don't like to eat and say out loud what you find revolting about it (for example, 'I don't like spaghetti because it's slimy', 'I hate crisps because they taste like salty cardboard').

3. Write down exactly the words you just said. It doesn't matter if you don't know all the spellings.

If you can do that, you can be a writer! It just means putting your thoughts and feelings down on paper; and you can do that as soon as you know how to write.

As you're reading this book, you definitely have more than enough basic skills. Most people have. So how come so many people who know how to write never set pen to paper unless they absolutely have to?

It's down to attitude. The difference between brilliant writers and people who don't write at all is in the way they think and feel about writing. This book is not about boosting literacy skills. Your teacher can help you learn lots of skills, but it's up to you what you do with them. This book will show you how to grow as a writer and find your own writing voice. Do this Quick Tick Quiz to see if it will be useful for you.

THE QUICK TICK QUIZ

Tick the statement that fits you best in each section.

SECTION 1

A I get plenty of practice at school so I don't do writing at home. ❑

B I write stories and poems in my free time. ❑

C I don't write things at home because I'm not good enough. ❑

D I don't write stuff at home. Why should I? ❑

SECTION 2

A Writing at school is important because you need it in every subject. ❑

B I like writing at school because it's fun. ❑

C I don't like writing at school. I might make mistakes. ❑

D The only good thing about writing at school is that it isn't maths. ❑

SECTION 3

A I mostly look up new words to impress my teacher. ❏

B I mostly look up new words because I want to know what they mean. ❏

C I have to look up new words because I'm rubbish at spelling. ❏

D I know plenty of words already, thank you very much. ❏

SECTION 4

A I don't see any point in writing things that no-one's going to mark. ❏

B I love it when my writing makes someone laugh or cry. ❏

C No-one would want to read anything that I might want to write. ❏

D I'm not bothered about writing and I'm only reading this book because my teacher's making me. ❏

RESULTS

Mostly As You've probably got loads of literacy skills – what a shame you aren't using them more! This book will get you started.

Mostly Bs You're already a brilliant writer. You don't need any tips from me! But read on anyway – you'll probably love this book because you love everything to do with reading and writing.

Mostly Cs You worry too much! Read on to find out how to enjoy your writing more.

Mostly Ds You tell it how it is – I like that! Stroppy people often make great writers because they've got a lot to say for themselves. Surprise yourself – read on!

Author tip

What's great about writing? Being able to do it in your pyjamas!

Catherine Johnson, author of *Face Value* (Oxford University Press, 0-1927-5406-8)

2. PMA – and what gets in the way

Football coaches and athletics trainers know how important it is to have a Positive Mental Attitude, and doctors have found that ill people who have a Positive Mental Attitude actually get better quicker.

In fact, a Positive Mental Attitude will help you to achieve anything you set out to do – including being a brilliant writer – and a Negative Mental Attitude will hold you back.

> **"Whether you think that you can, or that you can't, you are usually right."**
> Henry Ford, founder of the Ford Motor Company

How you think about something affects how you feel about it. How you feel about it affects how much you do it. How much you do something affects how well you do it, because practice makes perfect. Check out these diagrams to see how it works.

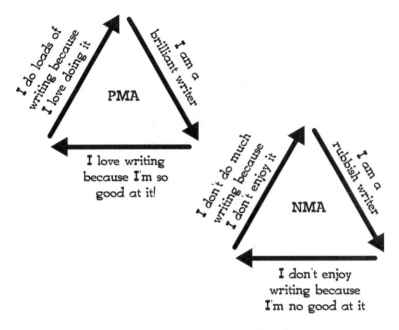

A surprising number of people think that they're no good at writing – so where does this Negative Mental Attitude come from? Quite often it comes from the crazy idea that writing is the same as literacy.

Writing is not the same as literacy!

Literacy is about the nuts and bolts of writing, and you can measure how good or bad you are at it. Maybe you can do apostrophes – excellent! – maybe you can't get the hang of complex sentences – must try harder! But writing is not about tests and standards – it's about expressing yourself and developing your own unique writing voice.

You can like or dislike someone's writing voice but you can't judge it, any more than you would judge a person's speaking voice, because it's just part of who they are.

I asked the Thompson family to write something on the subject of toast (I didn't really – I made them up – but it sounds good, doesn't it?)

Which one do you think is the best writer?

Toast by Annabel Thompson, age 10.

When I get up in the morning I usually feel hungry, so I make myself 2 slices of toast. White sliced bread is best for toast because if you have to cut the bread yourself the slices can sometimes be too thick and then they get stuck in the toaster.

Toast by Jamie Thompson, age 11.

eating toast is like writing a poem. You feel hungry. You warm up the bread. It smells lovely. The butter melts on it. The butter is yellow, my best colour. You eat the toast. Then you arnt hungry any more.

Toast by Louis Thompson, age 8

How do porkypines cudle?
Very carefuly! Ha ha!

Toast by Maisie Thompson, age 4

The answer is – they're all the best! Annabel has the best literacy skills, but Jamie has the most unusual idea. Louis can't keep to the subject, but he's funny, and Maisie is the best at doing four-year-olds' writing.

The Thompsons can all write brilliantly, and so can you. Your writing is brilliant because it's brilliantly you, just as my writing is brilliantly me.

So if you think that you can't write – think again! Take a Positive Mental Attitude towards your writing. Don't be put off if you can't write like your favourite author or your friend who does descriptions to die for – remember, they can't write like you!

You can start right now by doing the PMA power pic.

THE PMA POWER PIC

1. Take a large sheet of paper and write in the middle:

I AM A BRILLIANT WRITER!

2. Get some scraps of coloured paper – bits torn out of magazines will do fine. Write and complete one of the following sentences on each one:

I love...
I hate...
I wish...
My favourite animal is...
My favourite colour is...
I remember...
My best friend is called...

When I'm happy I...
When I'm sad I...
When I grow up I want to be...
... makes me cringe
... makes me laugh
... makes me blush

3. Find some pictures of things you like or dislike, and some old family photos.

4. Stick your scraps and pictures all around I AM A BRILLIANT WRITER. If it seems like boasting, you can stick them over the top – you know it's there!

5. Put your power pic on the wall, and keep adding things as they occur to you (What I would like for Christmas is… I like *The Simpsons* because…)

Your PMA power pic is a celebration of you. It shows you how much you've got to write about, and gets you started on the way to being a brilliant writer.

Author tip

What's great about writing is that every time you write a story or a poem, only you could have written it. No-one in the entire history of writing will ever have put those words together in exactly that order.

Linda Newbery, author of *At the Firefly Gate* (Orion, 1-8425-5195-7) www.lindanewbery.co.uk

3. How to handle criticism

It can feel like a risky business showing your writing to other people because you are opening yourself up to criticism. Sometimes you can't avoid it, for example at school. And you shouldn't avoid it!

Author tip

There is one person in particular you must try to please with your writing. Yourself.

Linda Newbery

Sharing adds a whole new dimension to your writing, bringing fresh ideas and feedback, as well as the pleasure of seeing the effect your words can have on other people. The problem is that if you don't know how to handle criticism, other people's opinions can sometimes make you feel like giving up altogether!

Do this quiz to see if you need some helpful hints.

QUIZ - CAN YOU HANDLE CRITICISM?

Your teacher writes this on your story: 'I like your hero, Hannibal Gercluckenbluffenblicker, but I did wonder if his surname was a bit too long? Great first name, though!' How do you respond?

My story's good!

My story's no good because I used a silly name

So why has he dissed the best bit?

But could it be better if I changed the name?

Nothing I write is any good

Hmm... maybe Gerclucken... etc doesn't really work

No, I actually still think it's funny

I'm going to chuck it in the bin

I'm not even going to think about it!

I'll talk to my teacher about it

But I'll change it if that's what he thinks

I'm going to stare out the window and sulk

I think I'll change it

He's convinced me

I've convinced him

I think I'll keep it

Oh dear!

You don't let criticism put you off – but you aren't exactly making the most of it

You're on the case with criticism. I bet your teacher loves teaching you!

You cave in a bit too quickly!

Make yourself a milkshake while everyone else reads on!

Check out my 5 helpful hints – right now!

FIVE HELPFUL HINTS

1. Be grateful for corrections

We learn by our mistakes, and learning to rite is no exception. when you hand in a piece of writing, you're teacher will mark the speeling mistakes and grammatical errers, so that you can see how to make your work even better. Maybe he or she will also point out other mistakes, like the fact that your hero's eyes, which were blue on the first page have turned brown by the end.

When you were learning to talk, your mum and dad had to keep putting you right.

> **More doosh!**

> **More juice, Bobby – say juice**

You kept trying. You didn't think, 'Right, that's it, then! I'm no good at talking. I'll just shut up!'

Be the same now as you develop your writing. When your teacher points out mistakes, such as incorrect spellings, keep trying and don't be put off.

However…

2. Be careful about suggestions

Make a distinction between corrections – where you've got something wrong – and suggestions. Your teacher might suggest you try something different: adding adjectives or making longer sentences, putting in more description, or cutting it down. The suggestions don't mean there's anything wrong with what you've written. They help you to think about your writing and be aware of the choices you make.

Although literacy targets might give you better grades for certain sorts of writing, that doesn't mean one style is better than another. My style is simple because I don't enjoy writing long sentences and descriptions. Some people think that's great and some people don't. For example, here's what three different publishers said about a novel I sent them recently.

'I like the writing here, I really liked the central character…'

'I'm sorry to say that I didn't ever take to the voice of Jaye…'

'It's certainly an excellent read. The letter format is accessible and poignant…'

It's a little-known fact that the first thing authors need to develop is a really thick skin! So try the things your teacher suggests, but remember it's your writing voice and what matters is that it sounds OK to you.

3. Don't play the all-or-nothing game

When you show your writing to others, you want them to think it's perfect, and if they find bits they don't like (which are almost always the bits you think are brilliant) you can go into a sort of free-fall of disappointment.

'She said it was too short... I can't write long stories... my stories are all rubbish... I'm no good at writing...'

Hold it right there! She didn't say you were no good at writing – she said that particular story was too short. Stop making a drama out of a comment and channel that imaginative energy into adding a few lines to your story. Sorted!

4. Notice the good

Don't just latch on to all those corrections and suggestions and gloss over the nice things people say. If they don't say any nice things, ask!

Say, 'Was there anything you particularly liked about the piece?'

One of my editors used to send me a long list of things she loved about the work and then add, as if it was an afterthought, some ideas about what I might change. That meant I always felt happy to go back to the text because I wanted to remember how great it was as well as seeing if I could make it even better.

5. Learn to be a good critic

The first rule of criticism is – make a sandwich!

If you've got something negative to say, put it between two positive things, like the filling between two slices of bread. Did you notice that's what the teacher in the quiz did?

The second rule is – be positive. Instead of saying, 'The monster wasn't scary enough,' say, 'I felt the monster could be more scary.'

And finally, keep it personal. Say, 'I think,' or 'I feel,' rather than just making bald statements. Instead of saying, 'That bit isn't clear,' for example, you could say, 'I got a bit confused at that point.'

Being a good critic means:

● your friends will be happy to share their writing with you
● you won't be too harshly critical of your own work
● you'll be able to deal with criticism better yourself

Your words speak up for you

I read a poem once that compared pieces of writing with brave soldiers going out to fight your battles for you. That's how it is. They are your voice. Don't give up on them if they come under fire! Welcome them back, dress their wounds, thank them for being so bold – and send them out to fight for you again.

the time in the world

OK

! Splash!

By the light
of the moon

GIGANTIC

that?

SOMEONE WAS COMING

It rained all day and all night

behind the curtain

( ) Yes! TAXI! forget a face. I never GO GO GO

Try to imagine

●●● (see diagram)

Hey!

Dear Auntie

ello?

a sudden

FEARFUL

No one lets

him join in

The
water
came
up to
their
knees

REE!

stic!

ne step

Then what happened?

All of

hmm

ars

are you?

But of course!

Let

What was that noise?

and, as if to prove it

WHY? WHY? WHY?

Part Two

You can start right now

1. The writer's kit list

What do you need in order to become a brilliant writer? Hardly anything!

BASIC EQUIPMENT

On the shelf beside my desk I always have:
- Three A4 loose leaf pads – one plain, one lined and one yellow!
- A heap of scrap paper
- A jar of coloured gel pens (the best thing ever invented!)
- A box file full of ideas I've jotted down – when I need a new idea, I empty it out and go through them
- A dictionary
- A heap of pocket-sized notepads

Author tip

Always carry a notebook. I do.
My best ideas often come from
when I'm walking my dog. I write
them down straight away so
I don't forget them.

Elizabeth Lindsay, author of
A Crack in the Dark Glass
(Solidus, 0-9543-3773-5)
www.elizabethlindsay.co.uk

Another tip is to choose clothes that have pockets
so you have somewhere to keep your notebook!

It's great if you've got a computer at home but
if you haven't, don't worry – Shakespeare managed
fine without one.

SOME LANGUAGE SKILLS

You don't need much in the way of special skills.

1. Grammar - don't even think about it!

Grammar is how we put words together to make
sentences, and it comes completely naturally when we
learn to talk. So just write as you would talk, and then
check it sounds OK when you read it back.

2. Punctuation – it puts in the pauses

Full stops and commas put in the pauses that you
would hear if someone was talking to you. You need
full stops otherwise every sentence would be endless
your readers would feel confused they wouldn't know
what was going on. Commas mark little pauses within
a sentence, and it's partly a matter of taste how many
you put in, as it's a matter of taste how much salt you
sprinkle on your chips. You can check you've got the
pauses in the right places by reading aloud, just the
same way as you check your grammar.

Full stops and commas are all you really need
to get started but actually, punctuation can be fun.
'How can that be?' I hear you say, but it's nice knowing
where speech marks go and adding a few dashes here
and there – and then, you've got apostrophes and
exclamation marks! There are semi colons; there are
colons: use colons before lists, before quotations,

or just to split up a sentence. And don't forget those three mysterious dots…

You can put more pep in your punctuation by noticing how other writers use it in the books and mags you read (start now with this one – oh! I forgot to mention brackets! Aren't they nice?) and by paying attention in literacy lessons.

3. Spelling – don't get hung up about it

Lots of people get hung up about spelling, but why? You can always check hard words in the dictionary or use the spell checker if you're writing on a computer.

4. Wonderful words – start collecting them!

When I was little, my gran had a button box. I suppose the idea was that if you collected all the old buttons from clothes you were throwing away, you'd always have a choice of buttons to sew on any new garments you made.

Gran had little round pearl buttons and big brown coat buttons; white sensible shirt buttons and sparkly pink ones. She had buttons with two holes, buttons with four holes and buttons with no holes at all. I loved tipping them out on the table and just looking at them, putting them in sets, imagining where they had been and where they might still go.

Well, that's what words are like – beautiful, useful objects, each full of its own mystery and magic, and you can collect them like my gran collected buttons. Then when you want to make a new piece of writing, you'll always have plenty of great words to choose from.

MAKE YOUR OWN WONDERFUL WORDS BOX

1. Decorate a box or biscuit tin.

2. Think of three words you like the sound of, and write each one on a scrap of paper – something pretty like birthday wrapping paper for a word like 'ballerina' maybe; something green and sensible for 'wellington boots'; perhaps something strongly coloured and bright for 'accelerator'.

3. Put your first three words in the box. They are your seed words.

4. Whenever you find a new word or think of one you particularly like, add it to the box. Write the word on one side of the paper and the meaning, if you've had to look it up, on the other side so that you'll remember.

You could choose a new word from the dictionary every week, or write new words you hear on your hand and look them up later.

5. From time to time, turn your wonderful words out on to the table and enjoy them! You could sort them into piles and see if you can make some unusual combinations.

Another great way of collecting words is making lists of things you're interested in – for example, cars or flowers.

Then instead of writing, 'He offered her a lift in his car,' you could put, 'He offered her a drive in his Ferrari' or Porsche or Morris Minor, and your writing will be more vivid and interesting.

Illustrate your lists with drawings or pics torn out of magazines.

WORD GAMES

You can enjoy words in other ways too. Get a puzzle book with crosswords and word searches if you're on your own, or try these three games with your friends.

1. First letter, last letter

Choose a subject, such as places or boys' names.

The first person says a boy's name (or whatever you've chosen), for example, Darren.

The second person has to think of a name that starts with the last letter in Darren – for example, Nicholas. The third person has to think of one beginning with S, and so on.

You mustn't say a name someone else has already said. If you can't think of one, you're out. When no-one can think of another name, the person who said the last one wins and you start another subject.

2. Mystery words

Everyone writes two words on a piece of paper and hands it to the person next to them.

You take turns telling a short story that includes the two words you've been given. The others then have to guess what the words were. Obviously, you can't guess the ones you wrote down!

3. In the manner of the word

One person leaves the room, and the others think of an adverb (the ones that end in –ly)

They call the first person back and he has to try to guess the adverb by asking each person in the room to do something 'in the manner of the word'.

'Pick up that cup in the manner of the word,' he might say, or 'go to the door in the manner of the word.'

If the word is 'sadly', for example, the players will do as he asks looking sad. He can have as many guesses as he likes, but if he has to give up he loses.

You don't need expensive equipment in order to be a brilliant writer – you just need a pen, some paper and lots of lovely words!

2. Fitness and skills

Writing is like football. If you want to be a brilliant footballer, you can't just go out and play in league matches, you have to build up your confidence, fitness and skills in training sessions.

If you want to be a brilliant writer you can't just write set pieces that are going to be marked or even read by someone else. You have to build up your confidence, fitness and skills by writing some stuff just for yourself.

When you do writing training sessions:
- you can take risks and try new things
- you can enjoy your writing without worrying whether it's good
- you are finding your natural writing voice
- you sometimes get great ideas you can develop later
- you are enjoying doing the writing and not just what you have written (the process of writing and not just the product)

WARM-UPS

It's a good idea to start every writing session with some warm-ups. These only take a few minutes, and you can scribble them on any old scrap of paper – you'll be throwing them all away unless you happen to have a moment of genius, in which case you can put that piece in your ideas file for later. You will need a clock or timer.

Here are some of my favourite warm-ups.

1. Write for 90 seconds on the subject of…
Don't give yourself time to plan it, or even think about it. Get stuck straight in. Do one or two at a time on subjects such as television, chocolate, summer or trees. When you've done these…

2. List ten subjects you could write on for 90 seconds!

3. On the subject of lists, write a list of things you could write a list of, such as ten things that make you cross, ten places you want to visit, ten ways to eat a jammie dodger… Then start listing!

4. Think of an object. Write a riddle about it, as if you are the object. For example, I am long and thin, and you could hold me in your hand. I am a lovely colour. Some people would say I am the best thing ever invented!

5. Do an acrostic that describes an object.

Gorgeous colours
Ever so many different ones
Like liquid rainbows
Pouring on to the page
Every time I write
No-one has invented anything more
Splendid!

6. Take three minutes to write a series of sentences that are not linked in any way to the one before. Something like this: Dogs don't eat lettuce. 'Go away!' yelled Grandpa. It was a bit cold this morning. My watch isn't working. A cream tea means scones and jam and clotted cream...

TRAINING SESSIONS

These are a bit longer than warm-ups, but again, you don't show them to anyone. They're just for you. Here are some I like.

1. Describe an article of clothing you once wore. Take your time. Think about how it felt, how it looked, how it smelt, where you wore it, what it meant to you.

2. Think of an argument you've had with someone. Write what happened, using 'I...' Now change your point of view and, using 'I' again, tell the story as if you were the other person.

3. Write for ten minutes starting, 'I remember...' or 'If I was an animal...' or 'My favourite teacher...' When you've used up these openings, make some more for yourself.

4. Do an A-Z of Christmas. 'A is for Auntie Sal who always comes to stay. B is for Burnt, which the pudding usually is. C is for crackers, and I got some vampire fangs in mine last year...'

You can do A-Zs of anything. Family, school, TV... you name it.

If you do some writing training a few times a week you'll find it much easier to get started on your essays and stories at school or on any bigger piece of writing. It's also a great way of helping you to get over any blocks.

Author tip

Sometimes, when you haven't done any writing for a while, it can feel as though you're blocked. It's a good idea to stop and do some short writing exercises. This will get you back into the mood of writing.

Liz Kessler, author of *The Tail of Emily Windsnap* (Orion, 1-8425-5166-3)

LEARN FROM THE PROS

If you want to be a brilliant footballer the other thing you must do besides training is pick up tips and tactics by watching lots of games. If you want to be a brilliant writer you can pick up tips by reading lots of books. Branch out and make reading a big adventure by trying different authors and different kinds of books.

The best way to do this is by joining your local library. It doesn't cost anything, and that means you don't have to worry about whether you're going to like the books you borrow.

Try fiction and non-fiction, graphic novels, and audio books. Remember you don't have to stick to your own age-group – check out the adults' non-fiction, or pick up a picture book if you're feeling stressy and fancy something funny and sweet.

Is this one any good?

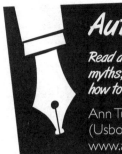

Author tip

Read as much as you can: novels, short stories, myths, comics. You will learn (without effort) how to write and how stories are constructed.

Ann Turnbull, author of *Josie under Fire*
(Usborne, 0-7460-6032-7)
www.annturnbull.com

You can also find lots of recommendations in *The Ultimate Book Guide* (A&C Black, 0-7136-6718-4), which lists more than 600 books, together with information about them, and ideas for other books you might like to move on to. You should be able to find a copy in the library.

Whichever books you choose, read a couple of pages and then, if you aren't enjoying that one, stop and read something else. Treat your library books like new people you meet – stick with the ones you like and steer clear of the ones you find boring.

Besides the library, there are lots of websites where you can read about books and sometimes post your own reviews. The website www.cool-reads.co.uk is full of book reviews by kids for kids, and so is www.kidsreview.org.uk, but you can only go on that site through school.

If you've particularly enjoyed a book, visit the publisher's website – the address is usually on the back cover – or check out the author's website to see what else they've written.

And why not set up a reading group with your friends, so you can talk about the books you've read? There's loads of stuff about starting a book club on www.cbuk.info or you could ask your teacher to help.

Wherever you get your reading ideas from, you'll want to keep a record of what you've read.

MAKE YOUR OWN AUTHOR FILE

1. Use an address book or label some file paper with the letters of the alphabet.

2. Record each book you read under the author's name on the appropriate page.

3. Give it marks out of ten for being funny/ exciting/ moving and add a comment or two.

4. If anyone recommends a book to you, jot it down in your author file so you'll remember to look out for it.

5. Dip into your author file to find books you can recommend to your mates.

Reading different things is the only way to find out what you really enjoy, and that will give you a big clue about what sort of writing you will enjoy too.

3. Get writing!

Some authors write sagas as thick as a doorstep, and others make up messages in greetings cards; some write non-fiction about dead serious stuff and others write funny articles for magazines. One sort of writing isn't better than another – they're just different.

To find out what kind of writer you are – write, write, write! Try all sorts of writing but, as with your reading, don't struggle on if you're not enjoying it. Stop and try something else.

Author tip

Keep enjoying what you write… then there's a good chance your reader will enjoy it too.

Katherine Roberts, author of *Song Quest* (Chicken House, 0-4393-3892-1)

WRITING A DIARY

Most brilliant writers keep some sort of diary, so why not give it a try? Use an ordinary notebook without the dates marked on it, so you can just write when you feel like it and you don't have to fit everything into a small space on days when you've got a lot to say.

Author tip

Write from your heart and write when you want to, not when you think you should.

Nicola Morgan, author of *Chicken Friend* (Walker Books, 0-7445-9897-4) www.nicolamorgan.co.uk

Add postcards, photos, pics from magazines, newspaper cuttings, cinema tickets, drawings... make it a real horde of treasure.

Keeping a diary is brilliant because:

● You're writing about your own life, which is a subject you really care about!

● It can help you to get things off your chest, like talking to a top mate but without the risk she'll tell everyone your secrets if you fall out with her.

Anne Frank called her famous diary Kitty, and she
started each entry with 'Dear Kitty' exactly as if
she was writing to a friend

● It shows you the special themes of your life – for
example, you might not have noticed before that
all you really think about is food/ friends/ football

● It shows you how you normally react to life and
what sort of character you are, from day to day.
(Are you a bouncy Tigger, a grumbling Eeyore or
a cuddly Pooh?)

● It's a great read, and it means you can look back
without letting your memory play tricks

Keeping a writing journal

A writing journal isn't just about your life. It can contain
any pieces of writing you want to keep. Use a loose-leaf
folder so that you can add bits and move things around,
and mark each piece with the date. Make your writing
journal look great by using different colour pens for
hand-written pieces and different fonts and colours
when you use a computer. Add lots of drawings,
decorated headings, borders and illustrations.

Your writing journal might include:

- Great jokes you've heard – you can tell them in cartoons if you like drawing
- Famous sayings
- Bits you've copied out of books – a lovely description for example, or an interesting idea
- Song lyrics you love
- Recipes and other instructions, such as 'How to clean your football boots' or 'How to stay on-side'
- Information – bus times to your best mate's house, where to find the best bargains, team fixtures and match results
- Your own poems
- Other pieces of writing – descriptions of people and places, film reviews, sporting commentaries

You can keep your writing journal to yourself but, as it isn't personal like a diary, you can also share it with other people. Then you might like to include quizzes, word games and surveys you can try out on your friends. You can also talk about ideas, and even write your journals together.

Writing for other people

Writing for other people is fun in a completely different way from writing a diary or journal.

When I was a kid we had a message wall at home where we could stick up notes to each other, or poems, or jokes – sometimes, our mates even joined in (the message wall was in the loo, so pretty well everyone who came to the house saw it!)

OTHER WAYS OF SHARING WRITING

1. Make a family newspaper

All family members can collect items which particularly interest them. Then at the end of every month, everyone gives their news reports/ recipes/ problem page/ whatever to the editor (which could be you) who puts it all together.

2. Keep a holiday diary or scrapbook

Each member of the family could keep a diary of a holiday to share at the end when you arrive home (so don't include anything too rude or personal). Or you could all collect tickets, postcards and souvenirs and make a family souvenir which

includes bits of writing from everyone, plus a record of all the places you visited and the things you saw.

3. Make a magazine with your class

You could invite everyone to join in or just do it with a few friends for the rest of the class. You might decide to choose a particular theme, such as music or football, and ask contributors to write about their favourite personality, or type of music.

You could include pieces describing how to become a great footballer or musician, or check out whether any great names once lived in your area. Another idea would be to write a guide to your school or local area for newcomers.

4. Start a writing group

You could do this at home if your friends live nearby or ask your teacher if you can stay in at break time to do it. Take turns to read your own work out loud, setting a limit of about four minutes max (it's best if everyone practises on their own first). Talk about the work, but always remember the feedback sandwich.

5. Visit children's writing websites

On websites such as www.kidauthors.com and www.kidpub.com you can post your own work and read things by other people.

6. Email, text and chat to your friends on line

7. Write letters

These could be letters to authors, artists, celebrities, politicians, footballers – anyone you find interesting. Tell them why you like their book, education policy, horse-dung sculpture, etc.

Enclose a stamped, addressed envelope and ask for a signed photo, then they're more likely to reply. Plus, you can make a celebrity gallery of photos on your bedroom wall.

Writing for yourself and other people can be a really enjoyable part of your everyday life, even if you don't like writing stories and stuff at school. But if you think you might be interested in writing brilliant stories too, read on!

like a dream

I climbed as high as I could

&

Yeah, right.

How are you?

the spider

two tickets to Mars!

the strangest dream

Yeah, whatever

Oh!

the boy sprang to his feet

Nada

THE LION ROARED

*****

Au revoir

oh really?

"Let's eat," said Frank, licking his lips hungrily.

Yes, master!

I had the strangest dream

Boo!

SURPRISE

disguised as a

Why didn't I think of that?

FUNNY HA HA

"Can

How could any

TO BE CONTINUED

Part Three

You can write a brilliant story

1. Just imagine...

Stories are everywhere, for example:

● On TV – including news stories, soaps, dramas and sitcoms
● In books – including novels, short stories, myths and fairy tales
● In magazines and newspapers

You could simply retell a story you've seen, and hardly use your imagination at all. Your own life is made up of stories, and you could retell those without using much imagination either. Today, for example, my stories include 'Shintie gets stressed at the vet's' – but if the vet was writing it she would probably call it, 'Vet stressed out by bad-tempered rabbit!'

Author tip

Lots of us authors write about similar things yet every story is unique. So remember it's your view of something that counts.

Ann Bryant, author of *Step Chain* series (Egmont Books)
www.annbryant.co.uk

Keeping a diary is one way of noticing the stories in your life. Here's another.

MAKING A STORY CIRCLE

1. Get together with some mates.

2. Take it in turns to tell stories.
Here are some ideas:

- My favourite toy when I was little
- My worst holiday disaster
- The first time I saw the sea
- An embarrassing moment
- My best-ever present
- The person I'd most like to meet
- I was most scared when...
- A family outing
- Anything else you can come up with!

Rules

Keep it brief – you don't want anyone dozing off! Do not share anything upsetting or painful; it's just a bit of fun.

These real-life stories are great to write down, as well as telling them to your friends.

When you've written one story, play around with it a bit. Try writing it again:

● giving yourself superhero powers
● adding a fabulous new character, such as an angel or a dragon or your favourite sports star
● changing the ending

Starting from real life is an easy way to get your imagination into gear.

What if you don't have much imagination?

Some people say they don't have much imagination, but actually, we've all got great imaginations and we use them all the time.

Suppose I told you I've just seen a hedgehog on the lawn outside my window – you would straight away make a mental image of the hedgehog and the lawn, because words make us create pictures in our minds, without even noticing it.

Here's half a lemon. Can you picture it? Take your time. What colour is it? Now hold it in your hand. Feel the soft fruit in its cup of cool, dimpled skin. Put it up to your mouth. Can you taste it? See how powerfully your imagination can create something out of nothing but words? (Now wipe up your dribbles!)

WAYS TO SPARK YOUR IMAGINATION

1. Creative visualisation

This is a posh way of saying daydreaming – but you
do it deliberately, instead of just drifting off when you're
bored. The key is to relax and not rush it. Pay attention
to all your senses. Notice how things feel to the touch,
how they look and smell and taste; what sounds you
can hear. Here's one you can try.

The mystery house

● You're walking down the road you live in. What's the
weather like? Is anyone around? At the corner, you see a
house you've never noticed before. It has a high hedge.
● There's a hole in the hedge. How big is the hole?
You push the leaves apart to look through. What does
the hedge feel like?
● Now you can see into the garden. Is it tidy and well
kept? Is it overgrown? Are there many flowers?
● Suddenly, you realise someone is in the garden. He's
watching you. How old is he? What does he look like?
● He turns and walks towards the house. He wants
you to follow him. Why? Are you going to go?

Isn't it great?

Author tip

Writing is great because I can stare out of the window for as long as I like and still say I'm working! I'm not just looking at the garden though, I'm wandering through a different world, with all my friends from the book I'm writing.

Cindy Jeffries, author of *Rising Star*
(Usborne, 0-7460-6118-8)
www.cindyjefferies.co.uk

2. Secret histories

This is a good one for people who like to start with something more solid to get their ideas flowing.

What's your story?

● Choose an object you can hold in your hands – maybe a stone or shell from outside, or something old that's lying around the house.

● Examine it and then close your eyes and use your other senses. Turn it over in your hands, feeling its shape and all its surface textures. Does it have a smell? Does it make a sound?

● Imagine where your object came from originally, and where it has been. Who else might have held it in their hands? If it could see, what would it have seen? If it could talk, what stories might it tell?

3. Music

Some songs tell a story which you can visualise and imagine, but listening to any music can make you feel emotional, and strong emotions will set your imagination going.

Listening to something really rocky will get your heart thumping and fill you with energy – just what you need to put you in the mood for writing action stories with lots of blood and guts.

See how love songs and sad songs make you feel, and what kind of stories they put you in the mood for writing. Be adventurous! Experiment with music you don't usually listen to, even stuff you don't really like.

4. What if...?

'What if?' is like a magic key that can unlock the imagination and open the door to a brilliant story.

Take anything from real life and ask yourself
'What if?' What if dogs… wore dresses?
There could be dogs' fashion parades…
it could be rude for a dog to be nude!

Here are some what ifs for you.

List five things that might happen if:

- An elephant escaped from the zoo next door
  to your school
- Your mum won the lottery
- The country was invaded by giant ladybirds

Author tip

*Spend some time every day doing nothing at all.
I'm glad I was sometimes bored as a child so
I had to entertain myself with what-if thoughts.
What if that teacher was an alien trying to bore
me to sleep so he could kidnap me and take me to
his planet? That's what's really great about writing –
entertaining yourself as well as other people.*

Julia Jarman, author of *Ollie and the Bogle*
(Andersen Press, 1-8427-0039-1) www.juliajarman.com

Using your imagination just means playing with ideas,
and the whole idea of playing is, it's fun! You use your
imagination all the time without even noticing it, but
when you notice it and work with it, the stories just
come bursting through.

2. Planning

There are three stages in writing a story – planning, the first draft and finishing off. These are otherwise known as the 'messing about' stage, the 'phew, it works' stage and the 'getting it gorgeous' stage.

Most people have a favourite stage, depending on what sort of person they are. Do the Which Stage is Best? test to find out which story stage you're most likely to love.

THE WHICH STAGE IS BEST? TEST

Think about how your bedroom looks right now. Tick the statements below that seem to fit best, as many or as few as you like. Be honest!

SECTION 1

Floor? What floor? No-one's seen that for a while! ☐
Don't everyone's drawers spill over? ☐
I must take those seven dirty cups downstairs. ☐
Hmm… The sweet smell of fermenting socks! ☐

SECTION 2

Floor's clear, but I draw the line at vacuuming. ☐
Don't open that cupboard door! ☐
The space under the bed is so handy for storage. ☐
You found a fossilized doughnut behind the bin? ☐

SECTION 3

You could eat your dinner off this floor… but don't,
because you might drop some crumbs. ☐
Of course nothing falls out when I open my
cupboards! ☐
Doesn't everyone label their shelves? ☐
That's enough tick-testing – I've got dusting to do! ☐

RESULTS

If you got most ticks in section 1: you don't mind
a mess – you'll love the planning stage.

If you got most ticks in section 2: you like things
looking tidy but you're not fussed about the detail
– you're a natural first drafter.

If you got most ticks in section 3: you like things
tickety-boo and you're prepared to put the time in
– you're a natural finisher.

The planning stage is like a messy bedroom because
it works best if you throw lots of ideas into the mix

and then mooch around in them. It's no good sitting chewing your pencil waiting for the perfect idea to pop neatly into your head.

Write down lots of subjects – floods, ghosts, teachers, shopping… Add some settings – home, school, the seaside, Africa… Throw in some character ideas – girl, boy, lizard, accountant… shy, lazy, angry, crazy… Pretty soon your head will be as cluttered as a world-class messy bedroom. But the right idea will surface like that clean sock you've been looking for – and you'll know it's right, because it's the one that suddenly grabs your interest.

Maybe at this stage all you know is that you want to write about a pop star who goes missing or an eco warrior trying to stop a road being built, but that's enough. Now it's time to develop some characters. Good characters are the key to good stories. Caring what happens to the main characters is what keeps you and your reader interested.

Author tip

I think one of my main points about writing is to create really good characters that you can believe in.

Griselda Gifford, author of *River of Secrets* (Andersen Press, 1-8427-0045-6) www.Griselda.co.uk

CREATING CHARACTERS

It's amazing how much you can find out about your character by simply knowing five things:

1. Their name.
2. What they look like.
3. Something they particularly like (a place/ activity/ person/ pet/ whatever).
4. Something they dislike.
5. Their special object – this could be a thing or animal they often have with them, a catchphrase or particular mannerism.

Take the main character in a book I'm writing – he's called Sam, he's 12 years old and he's got short dark hair, bright eyes and a quick smile. He loves football and messing around with his mates, and he hates hassle – he'll do anything for a quiet life. His special object is he's always telling jokes. See how much you know about Sam already!

Make sure you know at least these five things about all your characters, even the minor ones, before you begin writing. Just for fun, try doing it now for yourself – without thinking about it, jot down whatever comes into your head for each of the five things. When you've finished, do it for your family and friends.

Oops! Up pops the plot!

The plot comes naturally from the characters. Your main character has to start with a problem – otherwise basically he's jogging along perfectly happily and there's nothing interesting about that.

What would be a big problem for a happy-go-lucky character like Sam? In my story, I separate him from his mates and stick him on a tiny island where the kids his age are terrorized by an evil older boy. Sam can't just shrug things off with a joke and go for a kick-around there! The story comes out of his efforts to find a way to break the older boy's power.

Supposing your main character loves spending time with her mates. What could be a problem for her? Maybe she has lots of little sisters and brothers and no room of her own, so she can't have sleepovers, etc. You could just make her parents win the lottery and move to a mansion, but then your story would be over by the end of the first paragraph.

Your main character has to try different ways of sorting out the problem, and experience several setbacks before finally succeeding.

For maths-minded people, it looks like this:

Problem + setbacks + solution = plot

More arty types might
see it like this:

I-want-my-own-bedroom-girl might start by trying
to sweet talk or bully her parents into, say, converting
the garage. They're probably too poor from feeding
all those little ones to be able to do that, and all she'll
achieve is making them feel fed up. Could she try to
earn some money herself? Could she ask a rich relative?
Could she go searching for something valuable or enter
a competition? Yes! She could try all these plans and
more until she solves her problem.

A word about settings

Some people say you should only write what you know,
but if everyone did that we'd never have had Hogwarts
or Middle Earth. However, do bear in mind that what's
familiar to you won't be familiar to everyone.

If you live in a rambling old house, or on a farm,
or in a high rise flat, that will seem exotic and different

to someone who lives in a suburban semi. You don't have to make up places to be interesting.

Moving on...

How do you know when you've done enough planning and you're ready to move on to the next stage? Well, again – it's a question of what kind of person you are.

Writing a story is a bit like going on a journey. In the same way that some people will pack everything they could possibly need and others will just throw a few things in an overnight bag, some writers like to have every detail of the plot mapped out before they start and others can just invent a character and set off.

The only thing I would recommend is that you know roughly how the story will end before you start writing, because knowing where you're heading keeps the story on course and gives it momentum.

Author tip

Reading stories is great but writing them is even better. You're in control, it's your world, full of characters doing whatever daring tasks you give them.

Sandra Glover, author of *Crazy Games*
(Corgi, 0-5525-4803-0)

3. The first draft

It might be tempting to try to get your story perfect first time, so that you can avoid the extra work of rewrites, but if you think like that, you're going to miss out on everything that's so superlative about the first draft (guess which story stage I like best?).

The whole point about the first draft is that it doesn't have to be right – therefore you can ham it up, try things out and generally enjoy yourself. If it sounds naff or clumsy, you can sort that out later. The rule for the first draft is always:

Don't get it right – get it written!

You can limber up for the first draft by playing The Story Game.

THE STORY GAME

1. Get together with a group of friends.
2. Start 'Once upon a time…' and make up a story, taking turns to say one sentence each.

Note: if you like, you can decide what sort of story you're going to tell before you start – last time I played this, we told ghost stories in the dark – spooky!

Another note: sometimes you get to a really great ending, but otherwise, just stop when it gets too silly.

Yet another note: a nice variation is to do a quick-fire round saying one word each.

The thing about the story game is that you can't spend ages humming and hawing because then everyone else will get fed up and start throwing things at you. You just have to get on with it.

In the story game, stories develop through the telling, and in your first draft your story will develop through the writing.

The two things you are looking for in your first draft are:

1. The voice of the story
2. A structure that works

Both of these come naturally from the characters, so at this stage you'll want to get into character like an actor rehearsing a new part.

Getting into character

You know things about your main characters at the planning stage but now you need to feel what it's like to be them. Little kids do this in dressing-up games; you can do it by acting out your characters' body language. Is your hero happy? Think happy thoughts and see what happens to your body – sit back, open up, smile.

See what it feels like to mirror other people. Has the newsreader you're watching on TV got stern eyes? Make your eyes like that. See how it feels to be behind that sort of face.

How was your day?

Fighting broke out in the mathematics corridor but, according to sources close to the head teacher, calm was quickly restored.

Copying other people's body language is a great way to experience what it's like to be someone who isn't you.

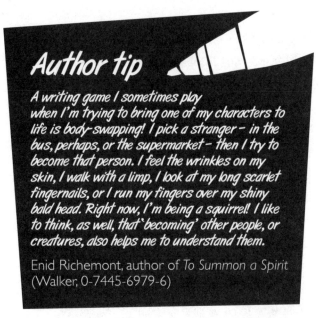

Author tip

A writing game I sometimes play when I'm trying to bring one of my characters to life is body-swapping! I pick a stranger – in the bus, perhaps, or the supermarket – then I try to become that person. I feel the wrinkles on my skin, I walk with a limp, I look at my long scarlet fingernails, or I run my fingers over my shiny bald head. Right now, I'm being a squirrel! I like to think, as well, that 'becoming' other people, or creatures, also helps me to understand them.

Enid Richemont, author of *To Summon a Spirit* (Walker, 0-7445-6979-6)

As you feel your way into your main character your writing will naturally find the right voice. If your heroine is a dreamy kind of person, the voice of her story will probably be quite poetic.

The sunlight dazzled on the water. Felicity looked down at the beach below, and it seemed to her that she saw him waiting for her there, just as he had been every day throughout the summer...

If she's a feisty adventurer the voice will be more active and down to earth.

Fliss stopped at the top of the beach and looked down. She thought she saw him, but it was just the sun in her eyes. What was going on? Why wasn't he there? He was always there, that summer!

Sometimes the characters will be happy to follow your plan for them, but occasionally they seem to take on a life of their own.

Feeling your way into feisty-adventurer-mode, for example, might bring in a flood of new ideas that you'd never have come up with at the planning stage. You might want to adapt or ditch your first plan and develop a whole new one.

Author tip

There are characters that you invent and then they thank you by doing something totally unplanned and ruining your plot!

Rosie Rushton, author of
The Secrets of Love
(Piccadilly Press, 1-8534-0774-7)
www.rosierushton.com

Reading back

When you've finished your first draft, read back over it and decide what you want to do next. You could:

● Keep it just as it is because it's already perfect.
● Bin it because it basically isn't going to work and besides, you've thought of a better idea now.
● Put it on the back burner – which means keep it in mind for another time – because it doesn't really work, but you still like some of the ideas.
● Redraft it and get it gorgeous!

4. Getting it gorgeous

Before you start, take a moment to enjoy the fact that you've finished your first draft.

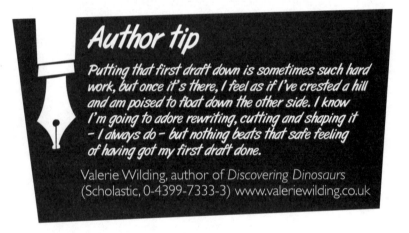

Author tip

Putting that first draft down is sometimes such hard work, but once it's there, I feel as if I've crested a hill and am poised to float down the other side. I know I'm going to adore rewriting, cutting and shaping it – I always do – but nothing beats that safe feeling of having got my first draft done.

Valerie Wilding, author of *Discovering Dinosaurs* (Scholastic, 0-4399-7333-3) www.valeriewilding.co.uk

Now here are five top tips on making a great second draft.

1. Write a blurb

The blurb is that bit on a book jacket that describes what the story's about. Read a few to get the feel of them and then try to describe your story in three sentences. This is a great way of focusing on what matters, and seeing which parts you could cut.
It also helps you to…

2. Decide what kind of story it is

Maybe when you started your first draft you didn't really know what kind of story you were writing – it might have turned out much funnier than you expected, for example, or maybe an uninvited ghost came wafting in. Before you start redrafting, decide what sort of story it is – then cut out anything that doesn't belong and make the rest even more:

● exciting if it's an adventure story
● spooky if it's a supernatural story
● funny if it's a funny story
● imaginative if it's a fantasy story

3. Mind your language

Reading your first draft aloud is the best way to check the punctuation and make sure the dialogue sounds right, and it will help you spot any accidental repetitions. Cut any unnecessary words and check you've chosen the best ones for the job. For example, see if you can replace adverbs with more powerful verbs.

~~'Get lost!'~~ Annabel said, ~~tersely.~~
She ~~went~~ angrily out of the ~~room.~~

'Get lost!' Annabel snapped.
She stormed out of the room.

4. Check the details

Your story will feel more vivid and realistic if you sometimes give details instead of being more general. For example, if your heroes packed some food before they set out, what did they take? The Famous Five usually took ham sandwiches and lashings of ginger beer! If your story is set in a town or city, what is it called? Make up names or use real ones if you've got a real place in mind.

5. Use your senses

Check your story to see whether you could offer your reader more information by describing what your characters experience through their senses. 'He went into the cave and turned on his torch,' is a bit blunt.

'He went into the cave. It was pitch black inside, and all the sounds seemed magnified – the plop of drips from the cave roof, the rapid gasp of his own breathing. The cave smelt dank and the boy began to shiver. He turned on his torch.'

6. Start in the middle!

One part of the first draft you can often cut is the beginning. So look at your first few sentences and ask yourself whether the story really needs them. Is there a moment after the beginning that would make a more exciting start?

~~Jazz lived in a terraced house near the railway line with his mum and dad, his sister Isabel and their two cats, Jack and Jester. Sometimes he and his mate, Big Pete, used to go to the bridge to watch the trains. One day, when they were up there waiting,~~ there was a sound like thunder, rumbling along the rails and suddenly the train came whooshing through. In the silence that followed, ~~they~~ *Jazz and Big Pete* saw something lying beside the track. They ran down off the bridge to get a better look.

7. Tie up the loose ends

Don't leave loose ends. OK, so your main character has succeeded in his challenge, but what about your minor characters?

Also, for a really satisfying ending, your hero should have grown and changed — often, he's had to find more courage in himself, or maybe he's learnt to be tougher or kinder or more patient.

Author tip

A story has two endings: an end to the action, and an end for the main character. What does your character think about or reflect on when they get to the end of all that has happened to them?

Penny Dolan, author of *The Ghoul of Badger O'Toole* (Scholastic, 0-4399-6874-7)
www.pennydolan.com

When you've got your story gorgeous…
…write another one! Writing stories:

● is a great way of entertaining yourself and other people

● helps you sort out your own problems because you've had some practice helping your characters to sort out theirs

● lets you experience things in your imagination that you could never experience in real life

Yes... No... Maybe.

What?

THE FUNGUS WAS GLOWING!

first things first

Put your hands up!

Can you ever forgive me?

me explain

in the sand in sandw

ered the rabbit, haughtily

me explain

The condemned man ate a hearty breakfast

put the sand in

C'est la vie

the journey had only just begun

VA VA VOOM

No!

what I mean is this

and

Don't go there

When?

DAZZLING

STAND AND DELIVER!

!!! HUGE

ABSOLUTELY

One nil!

END OF THE ROAD

IT WOULD RAIN FOREVER IT LOOKED LIKE IT WOULD

offer you a lift," he asked

ne follow that?

lliant, but mad THE ENI

Part Four

You can write anything you like!

1. The secret of fab non-fiction

Jokes, recipes, adverts, articles, horoscopes, reviews, letters, comics – there are just so many different kinds of non-fiction! Most of us read loads of it without even noticing, and you might find that you enjoy writing non-fiction more than making up stories.

The thing I love most about writing non-fiction is all the special features you can throw in.

SPECIAL FEATURES

Main headings break the text up into big chunks, and then you can divide them up into smaller chunks with sub headings.

Visual features

In non-fiction, charts, graphs, diagrams and pictures can carry information – and they look great.

Interactive stuff

You can use tick charts, quizzes, Q and As, puzzles and so on to carry information too.

Boxes

Very handy for top tips, hot hints, interesting facts, quotations…

And my personal favourite, bullets.

You can use bullets if you:

● want to make several points
● just like the look of them on the page (aren't they nice?)
● fancy a change from using letters and numbers, as in…

THREE STEPS TO GREAT NON-FICTION WRITING

1. Research

This is like the planning stage in story-making, when you gather loads of ideas and just live with them like a messy bedroom until a nice tidy plan starts to emerge. But non-fiction ideas don't come from your imagination.

Non-fiction ideas come from:

- Your own experience – everyone is an expert in something. Do you keep a pet? Go on camping holidays? Have a favourite sport or hobby? Have you ever won a big competition or done something for charity? Are you part of a big family, or an only child?
- People you know – remember, they're experts too
- Books and magazines
- The net

One of the great things about writing non-fiction is that it shows you how interesting your life is. Another great thing is that it helps you to increase your knowledge.

Author tip

My advice on how to become a writer is to have lots of fun so you have lots to write about.

Ruth Symes, author of
The Mum Trap (Andersen
Press, 0-8626-4933-1)
www.ruthsymes.com

2. The first draft

As in story writing, the first draft in non-fiction is an experiment to find a structure that works. I usually cut up all my pages of notes into single ideas and arrange them under half a dozen headings on my study floor like a jigsaw puzzle. If that doesn't work, I make up some more headings and try again. When I've found a pattern that looks OK, I start writing.

By the time you've finished the first draft, you can see not only how it will work but also how it will sound. A lot of non-fiction doesn't have an author voice, for example, but when I'm writing books like this one I imagine I'm having a conversation with my readers, and so I do say 'I' and talk about my own experience.

3. The second draft

The second draft is a cutting and adding process like the second draft of story writing. Take out anything that's irrelevant – for example, if you've managed to find a good illustration, remember a picture is worth a thousand words, so do you still need all those words?

Add explanations and examples if your ideas could be clearer or you want to back up your statements with evidence, plus any new stuff you might have found out since you started writing. Read the whole thing aloud to help you get the punctuation right and make sure the writing flows.

Oh… I nearly forgot!

I called this chapter 'The secret of fab non-fiction' so here it is:

Only write about things you care about!

Pah! I hear you say. If only! Because sometimes at school, it might seem as though you don't have much choice in what you write about. Then the challenge is to find an angle, a way to make the subject interesting to you. Have you got to write about the Ancient Egyptians? If you find all those weird gods and goddesses just too strange, but you like cooking, how about researching what the Egyptians liked to eat?

Make a list of all the things that fire you up, your sports and hobbies, special places, secret ambitions… when you really care about a subject you can make fab non-fiction that almost seems to write itself!

2. Playing with poems

A piece of prose is like a walk on the beach – you stroll along, noticing maybe a bird here or a pebble there, getting a general impression. But a poem is like a shell you can pick up in your hand – you can feel its whole shape and see all its colours, and if you put it close to your ear you can hear the sound of the sea.

Because most poems are much shorter than prose pieces:

● You can use them to express a single thought or feeling, a memory or anecdote that can be real or made up, or even a joke
● You can use them like a snapshot to describe a person or place

- They can be dead quick to write, so you can run one off on the bus, or at the back of the class
- They don't take up much paper – you could fit one on a till receipt if you got a sudden burst of inspiration at the shops (a v famous poet, William Carlos Williams, who was also a doctor, used to write poems on the back of his prescription pad between patients)
- They're a great way to say, 'Get well soon,' or 'I love you'
- They're the perfect place for similes and metaphors

Similes and metaphors

They say a picture paints a thousand words – well, similes and metaphors are ways of creating mental pictures. You often find them in poems because there isn't room to rattle on.

I used some similes to start this chapter, creating in your mind the images of a beach and a shell. If I'd left out the word 'like' and written, 'prose is a beach you can walk along – a poem is a shell,' they would have been metaphors.

Here comes another metaphor now…

A POEM IS A PICTURE

The first thing you notice about a poem is what it looks like – in fact, that's sometimes the only way you can tell it's a poem and not prose.

Just set out the words
In a certain way
And they will say
Look at us
We're a poem!

You can play around with the look of your poems, changing the line lengths, grouping the lines in different ways or using different styles of writing.

Write the words big and they

shout!

Write the words small and they

whisper!

You can write concrete poems, where the words make the shape of the thing they describe, or acrostics, where the first letter of each line makes a word. You can play around with spellings:

Simile
when I spell simile wrong
i smile

And you can forget about punctuation altogether if you want to, because the line breaks show the reader where to pause. How cool is that?

Here comes another metaphor…

A POEM IS A PUZZLE

Writing a poem is like doing a puzzle that you build by spotting gaps, finding new pieces and taking out ones that don't fit.

Maybe you know what shape you're going for before you begin – say you're writing a rap or a haiku – but you don't have to. Start with your basic idea and then play with it, moving words and phrases, swapping one word for another, and sometimes you will pick up a rhythm that makes you think, 'Hey – this would work as a four-line rhyming verse!' or a sonnet or a cinquain. (That's why it's great to learn some formal structures in class, so you've got more to choose from).

But quite often, if you listen to the music of the words, the poem will start to grow into a unique shape all its own.

The music of your words

A single word can sound beautiful like a musical note. Listen to the sounds of the words you choose. When you say a word, does it make your face open up in a smile, like tea, bee, me, wheee? Or does it close your face down in a frown? Is it soft and mellow like a luxurious pillow, or hard as a cricket bat?

Author tip

Take a real interest in words and language. When you are reading through a draft, make sure that every word you have written deserves a place in your piece.

James Carter, author of *Cars, Stars, Electric Guitars* (poetry) (Walker Books, 0-7445-8635-6)

Some words sound like the thing they describe –
the whoosh of waves, the crackle of gunfire. That's
called onomatopoeia. Some words are long, like
onomatopoeia, and some are short like oh!

You can highlight the sounds of the words you
choose by putting them next to other words that
sound similar in some way. Alliteration – starting with
the same sound – draws your attention to a group
of words. For example, who would have noticed
Peter Piper if he hadn't picked a peck of pickled
peppercorns? You'll also notice that authors and
journalists often use alliteration to make their
headlines sound more punchy.

Assonance – that's when several words have the
same vowel sound in the middle – is ear-catching too.
A gloomy mood, a dream of the sea, a black cat on
a mat, some yucky stuff, a big silly grin...

You can create rhythms by repeating the same
word or phrase; you can create rhythms by repeating
the same sentence structure. If you like, you can make
your lines rhyme, and this works particularly well in
funny or story poems. Try The D-da, D-da Game to
see how rhyming naturally seems to lead to jokes
and stories.

THE D-DA, D-DA GAME

1. Up to eight people sit in a circle.

2. The first person says a line in this rhythm
(more or less!)
    D-da, d-da, d-da, d-da, d-da
    For example,
    A little hedgehog walking down the lane

3. The second person says a line that rhymes with that
one and goes on to offer a second line, for example,
    Met a mouse whose name was Liza-Jane
    The mouse said, 'There's a car – put on a sprint'

4. The third person finishes that rhyme and starts
another one,
    'You don't want to end up a hedgehog print!'
    But hedgehogs just can't run as fast as that…

5. Keep going until someone makes a satisfying ending.
    Splat!

Always read your poems aloud as you work on them because then you can hear their music better, and when they sound just right why not share them with other people? Read them to your friends and family, or see if you can do some poetry reading in class. Check out these two great websites too:

www.poetryzone.ndirect.co.uk
www.maninthemoon.co.uk

Poems can express a lot in a few words, but even if a poem doesn't say much at all, it makes you notice every word as a beautiful object with its own unique shapes and sounds. So write some poems now! Becoming more word-aware will help you to enjoy all your writing more, and do it even better.

3. Your brilliant writing life

Because most people first learn to write at school you can get the idea that writing is just something you do in school. What a waste!

And because you do SATs in writing you can get the idea that the only reason for developing your writing skills is in order to do well in tests. Excuse me!

All those lovely literacy skills you learn in school are tools you can use throughout your life to:

- have your say
- understand yourself better
- develop your interests
- entertain yourself and other people

The more you use them, the more your confidence and enjoyment grows.

So write now and write lots, and don't worry about whether it's good or bad or right or wrong. To be a brilliant writer you have to forget all about targets and tests and just enjoy yourself.

But there's a twist! When you do lots of writing just for fun your test results in every subject will improve all on their own, like magic.

Brilliant!